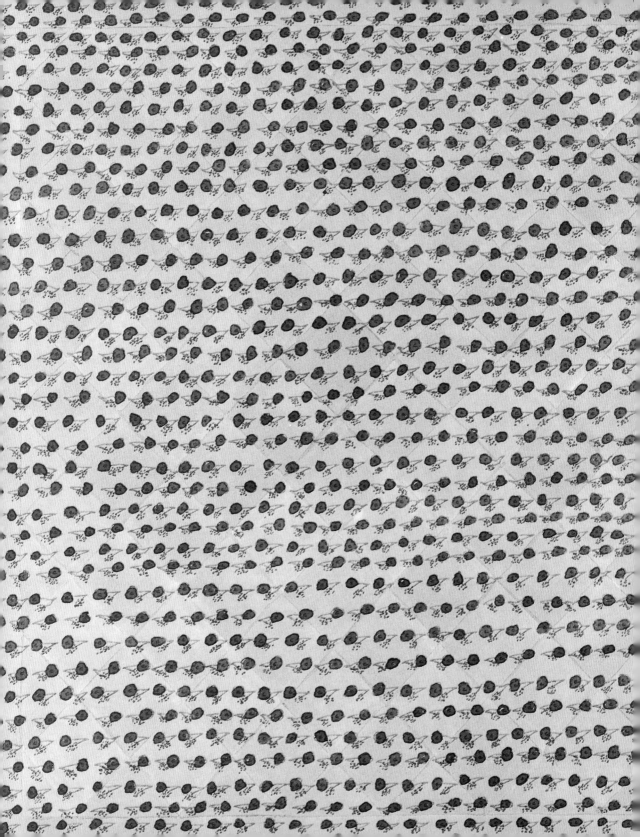

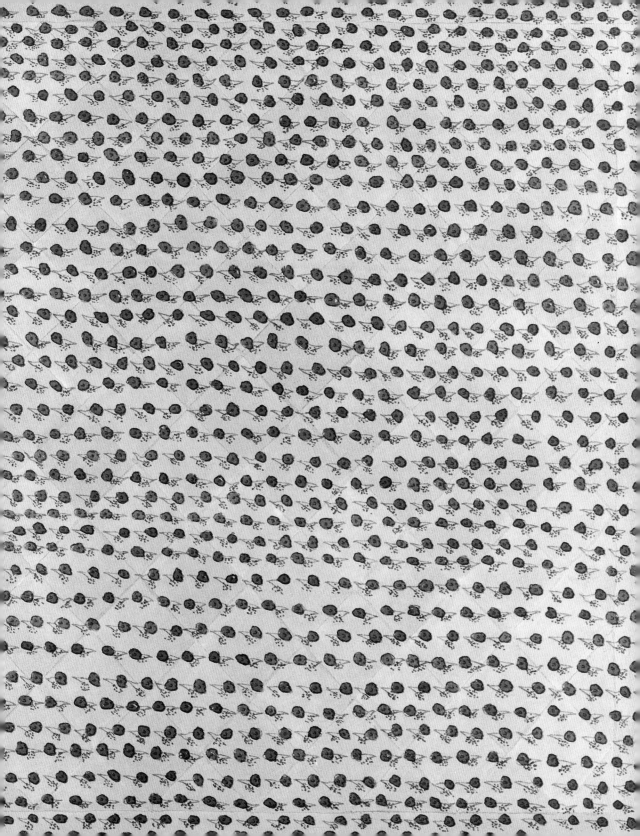

For Nina

Copyright © 1984 by Ann Jonas.
 All rights reserved. Published by Scholastic Inc., 555 Broadway,
New York, NY 10012, by arrangement with Puffin Books, a division of
Penguin Books USA Inc., 375 Hudson Street, New York, NY 10014.
Printed in the U.S.A.
ISBN 0-590-62353-2

1 2 3 4 5 6 7 8 9 10   2 3   02 01 00 99 98 97 96 95

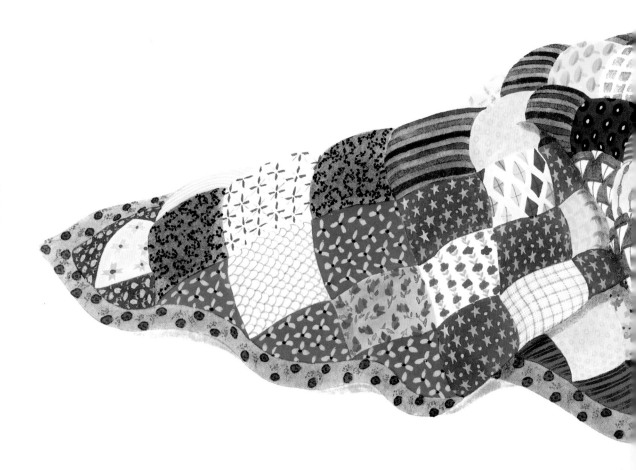

The Quilt
Ann Jonas

SCHOLASTIC INC.

New York   Toronto   London   Auckland   Sydney

I have a new quilt.

3

It's to go on my
new grown-up bed.

5

My mother and father
made it for me. They used
some of my old things.
Here are my first curtains
and my crib sheet. Sally
is lying on my baby pajamas.

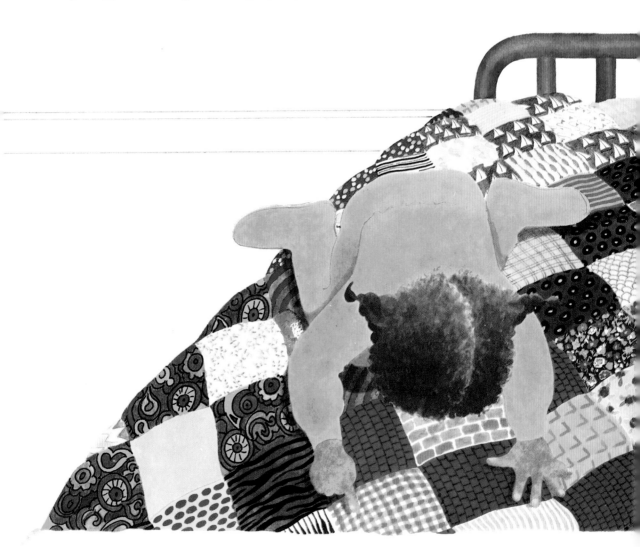

That's the shirt I wore on my second birthday. This piece is from my favorite pants. They got too small. The cloth my mother used to make Sally is here somewhere. I can't find it now.

I know I won't be able
to go to sleep tonight.

It almost looks
like a little town....

13

I can't find Sally!

Maybe she's here.
Sally!

16

She wouldn't like it here.
Sally!

What if someone
took her home?
Sally!

20

21

If she hid here,
I'd never find her.
Sally!

What a scary tunnel!
I'll run through fast.
Sally! Sally! Sally!
Sally! Sally! Sally!

24

She wouldn't be here.
She doesn't like water.
Sally!

This is worse than the tunnel!
Sally!

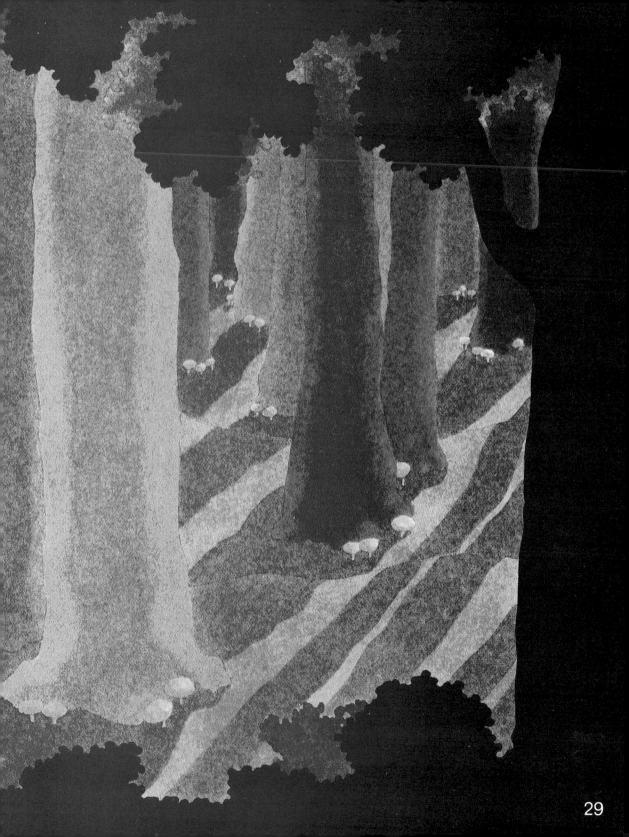

29

I see her!

31

Good
morning,
Sally.

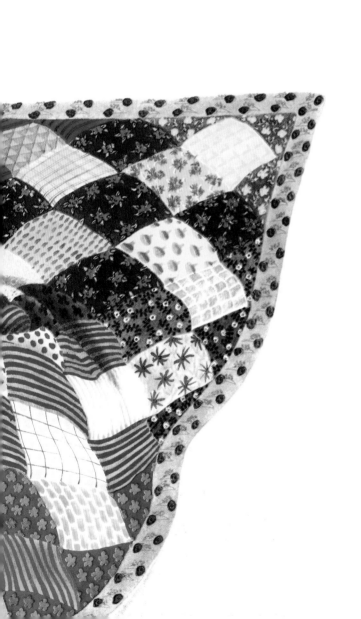

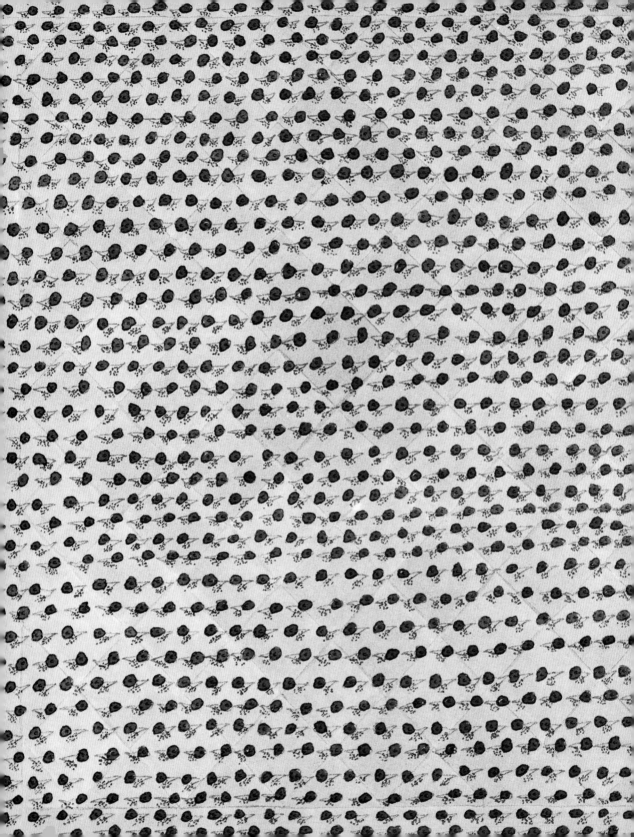

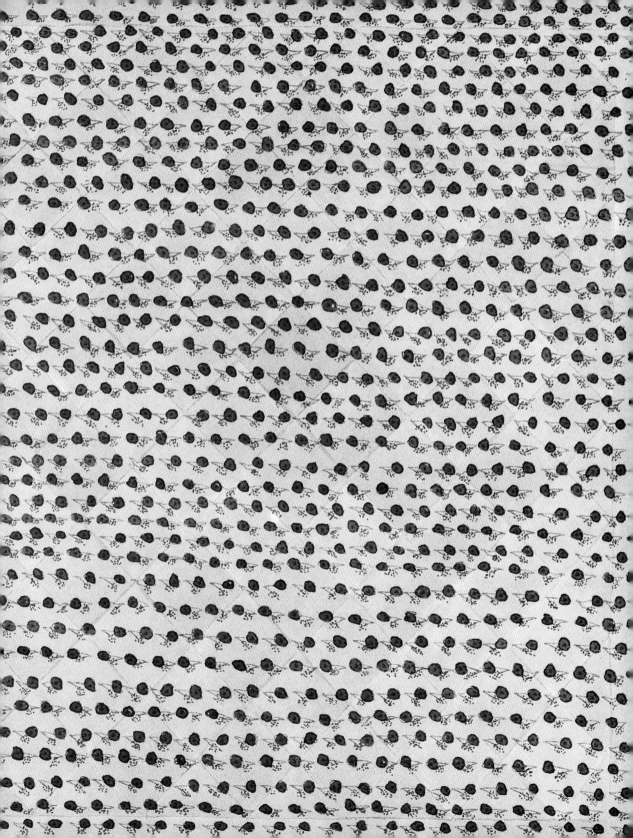